D1277945

An eager angel

"This task is a little complicated," said the Archangel of Persistence. "It could take a while. So if you want to stay and work on your tap dancing, I could ask another little angel to help out."

"Does the child need to learn persistence?" asked the Little Angel of Persistence.

"Yes."

"Then I want the task." The little angel stroked his wings in satisfaction. He loved all the tasks the archangel had given him so far. He knew he'd love this one, too. Nothing was better than helping a child. "Hey," he said, looking at his wings as if for the first time. "I'm almost fully feathered. If I succeed at this task, I'll earn enough feathers to finish off my wings."

The archangel smiled. "It will be a delight to hear the bell that announces your wings."

Aladdin
Angelwings
№. 16

Hang in There

Donna Jo Napoli

Aladdin Paperbacks

New York   London   Toronto   Sydney   Singapore

Thank you to all my family,
Brenda Bowen, Karen Riskin, and Richard Tchen

If you purchased this book without a cover you should be aware that this book is stolen property. It was reported as "unsold and destroyed" to the publisher and neither the author nor the publisher has received any payment for this "stripped book."

First Aladdin Paperbacks edition April 2001

Text copyright © 2001 by Donna Jo Napoli

Aladdin Paperbacks
An imprint of Simon & Schuster Children's Publishing Division
1230 Avenue of the Americas
New York, NY 10020

All rights reserved, including the right of reproduction in whole or in part in any form.

The text for this book was set in Minister Light and Cheltenham.

Printed and bound in the United States of America
2 4 6 8 10 9 7 5 3 1

Library of Congress Catalog Card Number: 00-062047
ISBN 0-689-83973-1

For readers whose pets understand.

Aladdin
Angelwings
№ 16
Hang in There

Angel Talk

The Little Angel of Persistence stood in front of the mirror and fixed his eyes on his own face. He wouldn't allow his gaze to drift down to his feet. He tried again: shuffle, ball, change. Those were the tap-dance steps he was trying to master. And his tap-dancing videotape said it was best not to look at your feet as you practiced the steps.

Tap dancing was fun, but it was hard. Dancing had become the rage among the little angels, ever since that new archangel had shown them all how to do jive. Jive was fun, too. And it wasn't as hard as tap. At least, the Little Angel of Persistence didn't find it as hard.

But there was something that made tap

better than jive in the little angel's opinion. Something that made tap simply wonderful. It was the intricate rhythms, the way a short pattern of beats could be added onto another pattern and another pattern, and then the whole thing could be repeated, and then slightly changed, and it could all just keep going in one big, glorious dance. Wow. When the little angel even thought about tap, he got happy. That was all there was to it.

The little angel tried again: shuffle, ball, change. He was slow and clunky at it.

He went over to the VCR and took out his lesson videotape and put in his favorite videotape of famous tap dancers. There was Fred Astaire, lightly tapping across the stage as Ginger Rogers smiled at him. There was Gene Kelly, giving perfect rhythms in the rain—even holding an umbrella as he tapped faster and faster. They both made tap dancing look so easy. And then there was the whole cast of that Broadway show that the little angel had seen in

New York City, *STOMP*, just pounding away, having a grand old time.

Ah, well. The Little Angel of Persistence looked at his feet. They didn't look bad. But no one had ever called him graceful. That's because he wasn't graceful. And he wasn't fast, either.

He sat on the floor and unlaced his tap shoes.

"Little angel, there you are." The Archangel of Persistence came rushing in. "Are you busy?"

The little angel put his shoes back in the box he kept them in. "Not anymore."

"Were those tap shoes you had on?" The archangel peeked into the box. "I thought so. I love tap dancing."

"Are you good at it?" asked the little angel.

"Oh, I don't do it. I just meant I like to watch it."

"That's how I feel about it, too," said the Little Angel of Persistence.

The archangel put her finger to her lips.

"But aren't these your tap shoes?"

"Yes. But I'm not going to use them anymore. It takes too long to learn, and I've got so many other really important things to do."

"What important things?" asked the Archangel of Persistence.

"For starters, the task that you have for me." The little angel gave a saucy smile and snapped his fingers. "Isn't that why you're here?"

"Well, yes," said the archangel. "But this task is a little complicated. It could take a while. So if you want to stay and work on your tap dancing, I could ask another little angel to help out."

"Does the child need to learn persistence?"

"Yes."

"Then I want the task." The little angel stroked his wings in satisfaction. He loved all the tasks the archangel had given him so far. He knew he'd love this one, too. Nothing was better than helping a child. "Hey," he said, looking at his wings as if for the first time.

"I'm almost fully feathered. If I succeed at this task, I'll earn enough feathers to finish off my wings."

The archangel smiled. "It will be a delight to hear the bell that announces your wings."

Playing Ball

"Time for gym." Mr. Moscatelli opened the classroom door. "Stanley, why don't you get at the head of the line and lead everyone there while I fix up some last-minute things for the fraction test, okay?"

Stanley was too surprised to answer—he had never been at the head of the line. No one ever asked Stanley to lead anything. But Mr. Moscatelli obviously didn't expect an answer, anyway. He was already erasing the blackboard.

Gym. Ugh. Gym wasn't great, especially on Mondays, when everyone seemed to play harder and faster than ever.

Stanley put his book and papers and pencil away. Then he went to the classroom door and stood there, while the rest of the kids lined up behind him.

He led the way down the stairs to the gym-nasium.

"Welcome," called Miss Lin, with a big smile. Miss Lin put a lot of effort into being cheerful, you could tell. She thought sports were the best thing in the world and she wanted all the kids to love them. She almost succeeded. Stanley had an undeniable urge to smile back at her even though he didn't want to be there. "It's volleyball day," Miss Lin said. "Volleyball!"

It took several minutes to divide up into teams and get the first set of players out on the court. Thankfully, Stanley got to stand on the sidelines at the start. Miss Lin swung her right arm up toward her left as though she was serving an imaginary ball. Her ponytail bounced. She recited the rules of the game and shouted out pointers.

Stanley listened and reviewed the rules in his head. Volleyball wasn't complicated. But somehow Stanley stunk at it, anyway.

Now it was Stanley's turn to rotate into the game. He stood in the center near the net. The ball whizzed over his head. This position was pretty safe—if he was lucky, maybe no ball would come his way. On the other hand, that wasn't the best attitude for helping his team.

Stanley turned around to face the rear, so that if anyone behind him hit the ball weakly, he could assist it over the net. Or, at least try. The ball bashed him in the back of the head.

"Why were you looking toward the back, Dink Head?" said Morton.

Stanley didn't answer. What was the point? His strategy was wrong. "Miss Lin, I feel sick."

"Sick? Again?"

"Yes," said Stanley.

"You were sick last Monday, too."

Stanley shrugged. "Can I go sit against the wall?"

Miss Lin gave a sad smile. "All right, Stanley. This time. But next Monday you'll play, right?"

Morton scored a point just then, and Miss

Lin cheered loudly and slapped him on the back. The game went on fine without Stanley, and Miss Lin didn't even notice that Stanley hadn't answered her.

Then there was math class, with the test. That didn't go so bad; Stanley could do a lot of the problems.

And then there was the ride home on the noisy bus. Stanley stared out the window and tried not to look like he was sitting alone, even though the seat beside him was empty, like always.

Finally, Stanley stood in the building corridor in front of the door of his apartment. Now this was the great part of the day. He slipped off his backpack. Then he opened the door and quickly dropped the pack on the floor as he pulled the door shut. He made a long whistle.

Casper came fluttering from the living room and practically dive-bombed onto Stanley's shoulder. Casper was a parakeet. The best parakeet in the world. He was albino, with all white feathers and pink eyes. Mamma had named him after Casper, the friendly ghost on TV. But even though Mamma had named him, Casper was Stanley's bird.

"Stanley. Come on in here for a snack," called Mamma.

Stanley turned his face toward the bird and bared his teeth. Casper skittered sideways on Stanley's shoulder and tapped his beak lightly on Stanley's teeth. That was their way of saying hello—sort of like a kiss without the lips. Now Casper climbed across the front of Stanley's shirt, hanging on with his little claws and his beak, and landed on Stanley's other shoulder. They kissed again, from that side.

Stanley walked happily into the kitchen. A bowl of freshly sliced mango sat on the table. Stanley bit off a tiny part and put it in the center of his left palm. Casper ran down his arm to his palm and pecked at the mango while Stanley ate the rest of it from the bowl. "Thanks, Mamma."

"How was your day?"

"Like always."

"That's good, right?" asked Mamma. But before he could answer, her back was already turned and she was washing up the counter and sink. "I had a good day, too. I finished writing that article on the baby gorilla at the zoo and I sent it to my boss, Mr. Schaffer, by e-mail. He just answered me. It's going to run in the Sunday paper. Mr. Schaffer liked it. He really liked it."

"That's good, Mamma."

Mamma dried her hands on the dish towel. "I've got to run a few errands. And, well, I need to get out and breathe some fresh air. Want to come with me?"

"No thanks. I've got homework. And I want to play with Casper."

"Okay. That little bird misses you all day. He's so happy when you're here." Mamma kissed Stanley on the cheek. "Mr. Lugassy is across the hall, if you need him. When I get back, we can make dinner together. Is there anything special you want me to pick up?"

"A bird treat. Maybe one of those honey sticks."

"Sure," Mamma said, and she left.

Stanley opened the drawer and took out a Ping-Pong ball.

Casper quickly jumped onto the table, ready for action.

Stanley flicked the ball along the table toward the bird.

Casper smacked it back with his beak.

They played ball fast and furious, and Casper had the time of his life, Stanley could tell, and Stanley didn't miss the ball once. Not once.

When they were done, Stanley went into his bedroom with Casper riding on his head, and searched through his basket of toys. The big rubber ball was near the bottom. He tossed it from hand to hand. It was about the size of a volleyball.

Stanley took the bird off his head and put him on top of the bookshelf. Then he went out the front door and down the back stairs into the courtyard of the apartment building. He bounced the ball against a wall and tried to hit it back with just his fingertips, like Miss Lin said they should do in volleyball. He missed it the first time. He hit it the second time, but it hurt his fingers.

Mrs. Rolfski opened her window. "Watch out, Stanley, or you'll break a window."

Stanley took the ball back upstairs. He didn't want to hurt his fingers, anyway. And playing with Casper was a lot more fun than playing alone.

Angel Talk

"Stanley is the child I'm supposed to help, right?" asked the Little Angel of Persistence.

"Of course."

"He's kind of an odd duck. But I don't think he's got any serious problems," said the little angel. "And I think most of his problems would go away if people would just listen to him."

The Archangel of Persistence straightened the hem of her sleeve. "What do you mean?"

"His teacher and the gym coach and his mother—they all asked him questions and then didn't wait for him to answer."

"Now that I think about it, you're right," said the Archangel of Persistence. "But they all seem to care about him."

"Caring is one thing; listening is another. No one listens to Stanley."

"I'm not sure that other people listening to Stanley has a lot to do with the problem I brought you here to help solve," said the archangel.

The Little Angel of Persistence squared his jaw in determination. "I've got to start somewhere. And that's the weak point that bothers me the most. So I'm going to make people listen to Stanley first. Then I'll go from there."

Artwork

Mr. Moscatelli walked up and down the aisles handing out packs of colored pencils. "Be sure to draw with an ordinary pencil first, so that you can erase if you need to. Then outline and color in with these."

Stanley looked through the pack of pencils Mr. Moscatelli had placed on his desk. The blue one was missing. Probably most of the packs were missing at least one color by this time in the school year. That was okay. He could draw something that didn't need blue.

This was a science assignment. They were supposed to pick something they'd been studying, draw it, label the parts, and then explain how it worked. What they'd been studying was cause and effect. And the way they'd been studying it was by looking at machines. That was the title of the chapter in their science book, "Simple Machines." It wasn't that hard, really, because the chapter was full of drawings. So all they had to do was copy one. The hard part would be explaining how it worked.

Stanley opened the book and flipped through the pages. He happened to glance over at Charles. Charles had already put a title on his page: "The Toilet Tank." Too bad. The toilet tank was the most interesting machine in the chapter. Probably every other boy in the class was drawing one. Stanley didn't want to draw what everyone else was drawing. He kept turning the pages.

The car brake. Now that was cool. And the clutch. That was even cooler. Mamma's car had a clutch. It was an old car, but the clutch was smooth as satin—that's what Mamma said.

Stanley set to work. He drew the flywheel first, then a long shaft coming out of it. Next he worked on the pedal. In the book, the foot pressing on the pedal was a woman's, in high-heeled shoes. Stanley didn't want to draw a woman's foot. He stuck his foot out in the aisle and used it as a model.

"You're going to make someone trip."

Stanley looked up.

Natalie sat across the aisle from him. "Did you just draw your own foot? On the pedal of a car? You're too young to drive." She blinked. "Besides, that looks like a gorilla foot."

Stanley blinked back. "You can't even see the foot. It's inside the sneaker."

"That's a sneaker? And look at all that hair on the ankle. It's a gorilla foot, all right."

That wasn't hair. That was supposed to be a sock with a design on it.

But now that Natalie mentioned it, it did look like hair. And she was right, the sneaker was hardly recognizable. And the shaft had a curve in it. And the flywheel was a mess. Stanley was no good at drawing.

He looked at Natalie. She was madly

18

working away. Stanley leaned out into the aisle so that he could see her drawing. It was a water pump, and it was half done already, and it was good.

"What do you want?" asked Natalie.

"You're good at drawing," said Stanley.

"Thanks." Natalie gave a little smile and went back to work.

Stanley raised his hand. "Mr. Moscatelli? Do we have to draw a machine that's in the book?"

Mr. Moscatelli sat at his desk, drawing something of his own with a ruler and Magic Markers. He didn't seem to hear Stanley. Suddenly he jerked his head sideways. Then he looked around the room.

Stanley waved his arm.

"Did you say something, Stanley?"

"Can I draw any machine I want, even if it's not in the book?"

"Sure. If some other machine really fascinates you, go for it."

So Stanley made a big X through the clutch drawing. He turned over his sheet of paper and drew a wheelbarrow. A wheelbarrow was simple—a simple machine. And it was easy to draw. And his red pencil was perfect for coloring it in.

When Stanley got home, drawing was still on his mind. He liked art; he just stunk at it. Oh, well. At least he could play with Casper now.

He dropped his backpack and whistled. No wings—no Casper. Stanley stood very still and listened. Yup, there was the little *click click click.*

Stanley ran to the kitchen door, dropped to one knee, and waited.

Casper came walking fast across the linoleum floor. He looked like a funny little man, his big belly swaying with each step, sort of like a waddle. There was something about the kitchen floor that Casper really liked. He'd fly anywhere else in the house, but in the kitchen he walked. When he got to Stanley, he hopped onto his raised knee, then hopped from there onto his shoulder, and they kissed.

Mamma came out of the bedroom. "Hi, Stanley. What happened in school today?" She opened the refrigerator. "Let's see what we have for a snack. Oh. What was that?" She jerked her head. "Did you hear that, Stanley?"

"Hear what?"

"I don't know. I guess it was nothing." Mamma looked at Stanley. "You seem kind of blue. Did something bad happen?"

Stanley sat down at the table and leaned his head toward his left shoulder, where Casper sat. The little bird was caught between Stanley's cheek and his shoulder—but it was a gentle kind of caught. Stanley rubbed his cheek tenderly on Casper's head. The bird rubbed back and gave off a nice seedy odor. "I don't like art."

Mamma reached into the refrigerator and took out a pear. She washed it and cut it into sections and put it on a plate in front of

Stanley. And she left the core sitting on the plate, too. Then she folded her arms and looked at Stanley. "What? How can anyone not like art?"

Stanley ate a section of pear while Casper attacked the core. "I don't know. I just don't like it."

"Don't be silly. Art is fun. Hmmm. . ." Mamma pulled open the low drawer that held all sorts of odd things. "Here." She set a long metal paint set on the table. "You used to love your old watercolor paints." She opened the case and examined the little cakes of dry paint with a smile. "These paints still look good. And the brush is in fine shape. How about you sit down and enjoy yourself for a while?"

Stanley got a grocery bag out of the bin below the sink. That's what he always painted on when he was little. He lay it flat on the table and got a bowl full of water. Then he dipped the brush in the water and worked the wet brush around on top of the blue paint cake.

What would he paint? Not another machine. Casper. He could paint a picture of Casper.

Stanley put Casper down on the table. "Okay, stand still, so I can get you just right. You won't be white, because I don't have white paint. But I can make you lots of fun colors." He painted the long line of Casper's back, ending in those three beautiful tail feathers.

"That's pretty," said Mamma. "See how much fun you're having? I'm going back to my new article now, okay? Call me when you're done." Mamma left.

Stanley painted Casper's head and throat and belly. He filled in the outline with green and yellow. But already the painting didn't look so good. Casper's head was too big for his body. And his tail bent down too steeply. And the paint wasn't even—there were puddles here and there. Everything was wrong. What was the point of finishing it? Stanley could start over on another bag, but that was so much trouble. He went to the sink and washed the brush carefully. Then he came back to the table to eat the last section of pear.

Casper hopped onto the bag and skittered across the surface of the painting.

"It's awful, isn't it?" said Stanley.

Casper kept skittering around the painting, looking at it from every angle. He seemed to be getting more and more excited. Good old Casper—he liked Stanley's painting. Stanley laughed.

That seemed to be all the encouragement Casper needed. He hopped right onto the picture of himself. He danced all over it, getting little birdy footprints everywhere. They looked like lace, or snowflakes. They were wild and beautiful.

Angel Talk

is teacher listened to him," said the Archangel of Persistence. "It took Stanley two times of asking the question, but his teacher did listen. And his mother actually waited for an answer about what happened during his day. How did you do it, little angel?"

The Little Angel of Persistence smiled. "It was a snap."

"Tell me."

"I did tell you." The little angel laughed and snapped his fingers. "See? I snapped my fingers by their ears. That surprised them and made them snap to attention, you might say. So they actually noticed what Stanley was doing or saying."

The archangel smiled back appreciatively.

"Nice. But, like I said before, I don't see how this is going to help. Even when people listen to Stanley, nothing gets solved. He doesn't get the idea that he should keep trying at whatever he's doing. He quit on the drawing of the car clutch. And he quit on the painting of Casper."

"I know," said the little angel. "But who really cares about a drawing? It's not like anything big depends on Stanley doing it."

"Wait a minute. Are you telling me that being persistent is important only about the big things in life?"

"It's certainly more important about the big things than the little things. Look at me," said the little angel. "Helping children is a big thing—and it's important that I be persistent in doing it. But tap dancing is a little thing. No one cares whether I learn to do it or not."

The archangel's face went sad. "Don't you care whether or not you learn to tap?"

"Sure. But no one else does."

"Listen to yourself, little angel. Are you saying you don't count?"

"No, but, well . . ." The little angel shook his head. "Now I'm all confused. Let's get back to Stanley. I think I'm beginning to understand you about him, at least. If drawing matters to Stanley, then he should work harder at it."

"I agree," said the archangel.

The Little Angel of Persistence rubbed his hands together. "All right, then. Stanley's going to have to speak up and tell his teacher or his mother or both of them exactly what his problem is. Then they can encourage him."

The archangel cleared her throat. "Do you think Stanley really knows what his problem is?"

"He's lazy," said the little angel. "Anyone can see that."

"Are you so sure?"

The Little Angel of Persistence looked at the archangel in surprise. "He said he was sick during gym—but he didn't look sick. I bet he said that just so that he wouldn't have to play volleyball. And he asked if he could draw a machine that wasn't in the book, even though there were lots of great machines in his schoolbook. I think he picked a wheelbarrow because it was simpler to draw. He takes the easy way out."

"That's sure what it looks like, isn't it?" said the archangel. "In fact, it would be natural to conclude Stanley's lazy." She moved closer to the little angel and looked hard at him. "That might even be the easy way out, wouldn't you say?"

"I'm not looking for the easy way out," yelped the little angel. "Don't say that. I'm just trying to make sense of what Stanley does."

"Is laziness the only possible explanation?"

"Well, I guess there could be lots of other explanations." The Little Angel of Persistence tapped his foot in frustration. His head was still spinning from what the archangel had said about tap dancing, and now it was spinning even faster. "Okay, I'll watch Stanley more closely and I'll try very hard to understand him. But I'm going to keep making sure people listen to him, because that can never hurt. And I'm going to try to make him speak up more, so they have something to listen to."

The Archangel of Persistence smiled. "That's my persistent little angel, all right."

Lunch

Stanley munched a carrot. The school cafeteria was full of friendly noise. People were talking to each other and throwing napkins and stuff like that. For an instant Stanley felt a pang of loneliness. Then he thought of Casper. When he got home, Casper would be happy to see him. They'd have fun, like the other kids in the cafeteria were having fun now.

Natalie sat down beside him. "Hi." She put her lunch bag on the table.

Stanley looked at Natalie in surprise. Usually no one sat beside him. "The bench is sticky there," he said.

Natalie stood up and looked at the bench. "Yuck. Did I ruin my shorts?"

The back of Natalie's shorts were grass stained, but other than that they looked fine. Stanley shook his head.

Natalie pushed her lunch bag across the table and went around to sit opposite Stanley. She held her sandwich in both hands and nibbled at the edges, rotating it in her hands, so that she nibbled all around the entire sandwich. Now she started on her second rotation of nibbling.

Stanley had never seen anyone eat a sandwich like that before. He picked up his own turkey and lettuce sandwich and ate slowly as he watched Natalie.

She smiled up at him with peanut butter smeared on her teeth. Then she put down her half-eaten sandwich and unwrapped a double pack of brownies. She reached over and put one in front of Stanley. "It's got nuts."

Stanley looked at the brownie.

"Aren't you going to say anything?" asked Natalie.

Stanley thought he heard fingers snapping. He looked over his shoulder. No one was there.

He looked back at Natalie. "Is this for me?"

"Don't be stupid. I put it there, didn't I?"

Stanley felt hot at the word "stupid." He didn't want to say anything else, but he needed to understand what was going on. "Why?"

"Because you saved me from sitting in the sticky stuff," said Natalie.

"But I didn't save you," said Stanley. "You had already sat in it. I just told you about it."

"Well, it's all the same," said Natalie.

Now that wasn't true at all. It wasn't the same. But Stanley didn't say anything.

"Don't you like chocolate?" asked Natalie.

Stanley did like chocolate. He nodded and picked up the brownie. It smelled good.

"Eat it."

Stanley ate. The brownie was fudgy and delicious, with just the right amount of nuts. It clung to the roof of his mouth in a wonderful kind of way. It coated his teeth and tongue. After he finished it, he moved his tongue around inside his mouth, cleaning off every surface.

Natalie waited. "Aren't you going to say anything?"

Stanley's tongue was still busy, but it didn't matter because he didn't have anything smart to say to Natalie, anyway. And, oh, there was that snapping again. He looked quick over his shoulder. Then over the other shoulder. No one was there. He looked back at Natalie.

"Well, if you're not going to do the right thing, you can just sit alone." Natalie got up and walked away.

Stanley wanted to call her back. What had he done wrong? But she was mad at him. It was safer to stay put. He went back to munching the carrot he hadn't yet finished.

Stanley opened the apartment door, and Casper came fluttering into his face all crazy-like. "What's the matter?" Stanley cupped one hand over the little bird and cradled him to his chest. That's when he almost tripped over the bags. Four of them: a bag of glass bottles, a bag of cans, and two bags of paper.

Mamma came from the kitchen with a fifth bag, brimming with plastic containers. "I'm going to the recyling center. Want to come?"

"Casper hates recyling day," said Stanley.

"I know. Casper hates any kind of reorganizing. Put him in his cage, why don't you? That'll help him calm down and we can go have some fun together."

"I'd rather stay home with Casper."

"But I was planning on getting you new sneakers. We could stop by Kohl's."

Stanley looked down at his sneakers. The heels were pretty worn down, but there were no holes yet. "These can last a while longer. I really don't want to go, Mamma. But I'll help you carry these bags to the car." He brought Casper into his bedroom and put the bird in his cage. Then he loaded the recyling bags into the car and waved good-bye to Mamma.

When Stanley went back into his bedroom,

Casper chirped loudly at him. Stanley opened the cage door, and Casper flew out past Stanley. He kept flying all the way into the kitchen.

"So you want a snack, is that it?" Stanley laughed and poured himself a bowl of Cheerios. He put a couple on the table, and Casper immediately set to work, pecking them apart. Every now and then he stopped and gave what Stanley thought was surely an appreciative glance. Stanley swallowed a mouthful of cereal, then he whistled.

Casper flapped onto Stanley's shoulder and nuzzled his neck.

"You always think I do the right thing," said Stanley. "And you like playing ball with me. And you like doing artwork with me." Stanley sighed. "Thanks, Casper."

Angel Talk

H e's not lazy," said the Little Angel of Persistence. "He carried the recyling bags to the car without his mother even asking."

"I noticed that, too," said the archangel.

"And he always does his homework and takes good care of Casper without anyone nagging him. So you were right," said the little angel. "Stanley quits for some other reason. Maybe he just doesn't like ball and art. After all, he even told his mother he doesn't like art."

"Did you believe him?" asked the archangel. "Think about what he did, not just what he said."

"Well, when his mother put the watercolors in front of him, he didn't protest. He started painting right away." The Little Angel of

Persistence wrinkled his forehead. "So I guess he does like art, after all." The little angel put his hands on his hips. "And, you know what? I think he likes ball, too. The other day he played ball with Casper, and then he went outside to bounce his ball off the wall, until the neighbor told him to stop. He wouldn't do that if he really didn't like to play ball. And when Natalie sat down by him at lunch, he looked at her a lot and he ate the brownie she gave him, even though I couldn't get him to talk much to her."

"You tried to get him to talk?" The Archangel of Persistence opened her eyes wide in realization. "You were snapping your fingers in his ears, weren't you? That's why he kept looking around."

"Yes. I thought that way I could get him to speak up. It didn't work. But, still, I'm sure he likes Natalie just from the way he acted. So he likes ball and art and Natalie—and he still took the easy way out with all of them."

37

"That sounds right," said the Archangel of Persistence. "So what's Stanley's real problem?"

"That's what's so hard to figure out." The little angel shuffled his feet in a soft-shoe step. "Remember the other day, when Stanley asked Casper if his painting was awful?"

"Yes," said the archangel softly, "I remember."

"He thinks he's bad at art. And at volleyball, too, I bet. And did you hear what he said to Casper this afternoon? About how Casper likes doing everything with Stanley. He sounded really sad when he said it, like he's lonely. Like he thinks Casper's the only friend he can have." The little angel gulped. "Maybe Stanley thinks he's bad at everything. Maybe that's why he quits."

"If so, he's very confused," said the archangel.

"Totally," said the little angel. "Stanley thinks people are either good at something or bad at it. He doesn't realize that most people have to work hard to get good at something,

38

whether it's sports or art or making friends. He doesn't understand persistence." The little angel looked at the ground. Then he twirled around and snapped his fingers. "I've got it."

"What?"

"They're the wrong people."

The Archangel of Persistence shook her head. "Who are the wrong people? And the wrong people for what? What are you talking about?"

"Stanley needs to talk to the right person, and he needs the right person to listen to him."

"And just who is the right person?"

"Someone who understands how hard it is for a kid to get good at something." The little angel smiled. "And I think I just might know who."

A Shoe

At morning recess Stanley hung from the rings in the middle of the monkey bars. He kicked his legs up and looped his feet through, so that he swung upside down by his knees. When Phil came up and wanted a turn, Stanley flipped his feet all the way over and jumped to the ground.

Stanley loved the rings, so usually at recess he'd play there, getting off whenever anyone else came up, then getting back on again when they left.

While Phil hung and pedaled his legs, Stanley looked around the playground. Natalie was playing freeze tag with a big group of kids. After a while, she stopped and went with two other girls over to the climbing bars. They laughed as they climbed. Just as Natalie reached the top, her shoe fell off.

Stanley heard snaps in both ears. He didn't bother to look around. Something was definitely wrong with his hearing. But he wouldn't worry about it now. Natalie was missing a shoe, and the right thing to do was help her. Natalie liked people to do the right thing, after all.

Stanley raced over to the bars. But by the time he got there, Natalie had already climbed down. They reached for her shoe at the same time.

"What do you think you're doing?" Natalie frowned at Stanley. She grabbed her shoe and shoved her foot into it.

"I was getting it for you," said Stanley. "That's the right thing to do."

Natalie was halfway back up the bars when she stopped and shook her head. Then she looked at Stanley again. "Thanks, I guess."

"It's okay." There were those snaps in Stanley's ears again. He shook his head to get rid of them. "Thanks to you, too. For the brownie yesterday."

Natalie still stood on the bars, ready to climb higher, but her face changed. She hesitated. "Why'd you shake your head just now?"

"Something's wrong with my ears. I keep hearing snapping."

"There's nothing wrong with your ears," said Natalie. "I heard it, too. A minute ago. It must be something in the air."

"Oh."

Natalie climbed down a little ways. "Why are you saying thank you now, when you didn't say it yesterday?"

So that's what Stanley had done wrong. "I don't know. But I did like the brownie. Thank you, again."

"You're welcome," said Natalie. "You're a good acrobat."

"What?" said Stanley.

"You know. You're good at the rings." Natalie's voice was full of genuine admiration.

"Oh," Stanley said in sudden embarrassment. "That's the only thing I'm good at. I wish I was the person my bird thinks I am."

"Your bird?"

"Yeah. Casper. He's a parakeet."

Natalie came the rest of the way down the bars and stood beside Stanley. "I know what you mean. My dog thinks I'm wonderful. He jumps all over me when I get home."

Stanley smiled. "Animals are stupid that way. But it's a good stupid."

Natalie smiled back.

Stanley spoke fast. "Want to do the rings with me?"

"I'm not good at them," said Natalie.

"We could go across the monkey bars."

"I'm not good at them, either," said Natalie. "How'd you get to be so good?"

"I don't know. I've done it for as long as I can remember. Even when I was too small to reach the bars from the top step, my mother used to lift me up to get started and I'd just do it. Over and over. The rings were my favorite from the start. On the weekends I go to the playground near my home and just hang and stuff."

"Well, you go back and hang now, and I'll stay here. See you later." Natalie climbed back up to her friends. When she got to the top, she waved at Stanley.

"Let's play something new." Stanley set Casper down on the little rug beside his bed. He reached into the bag of treat seeds and put a few on the rug.

Casper quickly opened each seed and ate the inside.

"That's not the whole game," said Stanley. "That was just to whet your appetite." Stanley picked up the seed husks and brushed them off his fingers into the bottom of Casper's cage. That's where Casper slept every night. Stanley cleaned it on Saturday mornings.

"Okay, now watch." Stanley put another bunch of seeds onto the rug.

Casper ran over to eat them, but Stanley whisked him up and put him on his shoulder.

"Wait. You'll see." Stanley took out his pack of cards and built a little house around the seeds with four cards, and held them all in place with a fifth card, which acted as a roof. He put Casper back on the rug. "Okay, now get your seeds."

Casper hopped around the card house, peeking at the corners, looking for an entrance.

"There isn't any opening," said Stanley. "You have to make an opening."

Casper waddled fast around the card house now. He gave out angry little squawks.

"Keep trying," said Stanley.

Casper flapped onto Stanley's shoulder and squawked loud.

Stanley laughed. "Don't yell at me about it. You're smart. Use your beak to pull a card away. Go on. You've seen me open doors. You can figure it out."

Casper gave one last squawk and flew

onto the roof of the card house. It collapsed under his weight. The bird gobbled up the seeds.

"I knew you could do it," said Stanley. "I believed in you."

Angel Talk

"All done," said the little angel. He snapped his fingers. "Just like that."

"Whoa," said the Archangel of Persistence. "What makes you think you're done?"

"Stanley understands the value of persistence now. You heard him talking with Natalie. He described how he went across the monkey bars and played on the rings when he was little. He talked about doing it over and over again. Even though he didn't actually say it, I just know he understood that it was all that practice that made him so good at it."

"How can you be so sure?"

"Look what he did with Casper when he got home. He encouraged the bird to keep trying to get at the seeds under that card house he built." The Little Angel of Persistence flapped the ball of his foot on the floor in front of him and slid it back in place slowly, like Fred Astaire. "Stanley even wants his pet to be persistent now."

"He may be talking right," said the Archangel of Persistence, "but I haven't seen him change his behavior yet."

"Okay," said the little angel. "I'll stick around until you're convinced. I don't mind snapping my fingers a few more times. And I can always knock off another shoe."

"Hey! Did you knock off Natalie's shoe?"

"Sure. And my plan worked. Stanley ran to the rescue, and they started talking." The Little Angel of Persistence shuffled in a circle.

The archangel watched the little angel. "What's that catchy little foot action of yours?"

"This?" The little angel turned his cheek shyly. "You like it?"

"Yes," said the archangel. "Is it part of another plan?"

"Nah. But I don't need a new plan. The old one is working just fine."

Gym Again

Miss Lin twirled the volleyball on the tip of her index finger. "Ready, everyone? It's volleyball day again."

Actually, thought Stanley, it's volleyball week. Miss Lin seemed stuck on it. Here it was Thursday and so far this week they'd played volleyball at every gym class. And when Stanley said he was sick, Miss Lin had told him that if he was too sick for gym, he shouldn't be in school at all. So she'd made him play. It hadn't been a pretty week.

But, oh, Stanley had a new idea for how to get through gym class alive. He looked around for Jacob.

Instead, he saw Natalie, right beside him, standing so close, he could smell the peanut butter on her breath. Maybe that was her favorite kind of sandwich.

"Hi," said Natalie.

"Hi." Stanley smiled at her briefly, then he went back to looking around for Jacob. And now there was that annoying snapping in his ears again. He shook his head.

"Do you hear it?" asked Natalie.

"You mean the snapping?" Stanley nodded. "Yup. You, too?"

"Uh-huh. What are you looking for?"

"Jacob."

"He's over there." Natalie pointed. "Why do you want him?"

"He's tall. If I stand near him, maybe we'll rotate into the game at the same time. Then I can take the position behind him, and the ball will never get to me."

"Good plan," said Natalie. "I think I'll go stand by Cheryl. She's second tallest." Natalie ran over to Cheryl.

Stanley was surprised. He hadn't known Natalie didn't like volleyball. That was something they had in common. And they both had weird ears—another thing in common. Stanley felt happy as he worked his way past the crowd on the sidelines to stand by Jacob.

Somehow Stanley made it through the whole of gym without touching the volleyball once. Natalie did almost as good; the only time she touched the ball was when she had to serve. And then it went right into the net on her first try, so that was the end of her turn. Not a bad gym day, after all. They smiled at each other in triumph when the whistle blew for the end of class.

Angel Talk

W hat are you doing, little angel?"
The Archangel of Persistence
didn't look happy at all. "Now both Stanley
and Natalie are looking for the easy way out."

"It's not my fault," said the little angel. "All
I did was snap my fingers in their ears so they'd
have something to talk about."

"What do you mean, something to talk
about?"

"Yesterday Natalie seemed to like it when
she found out that they were both hearing
snapping," said the little angel. "So I thought
that would be enough to get them going today."

"It got them going, all right. But in the
wrong direction."

"Who could know that Natalie hated volleyball, too?" The Little Angel of Persistence put

his hands on his hips and bounced on his heels in worry. "I thought she was a persistent sort. I was sure Stanley could learn from her."

"Why? What do you know about Natalie?" asked the archangel.

"Not that much, you're right. But she did work hard on her science drawing."

"True enough," said the archangel. "But at recess she gave up on the rings without even trying. She simply said she wasn't good at them. And now, instead of Stanley learning persistence from Natalie, Natalie's learning how to do nothing at volleyball from Stanley." The archangel ruffled her feathers. "You've just doubled your own task, little angel."

"What?"

"They both need to learn persistence. And since you're the one who put Natalie under Stanley's bad influence, you're the one who has to help them both."

The little angel felt slightly sick. He put his hands on his stomach.

"Oh, you're upset," said the archangel. She closed her wing around the little angel. "Don't fret. Two children need your help at once. But you're up to this task. I just know you are. I have confidence in you."

"You shouldn't," said the little angel sadly. "My instinct was wrong."

"What instinct?"

The little angel took the archangel's hands. "I thought the best way for a child to learn persistence was from another child. You see, when an adult and a child try to do the same thing, it's usually easier for the adult. So if the adult says to be persistent, it doesn't matter that much—the adult doesn't really understand how hard it is for the child. But if another child says to be persistent, that matters."

"That sounds like a good instinct to me," said the archangel tenderly. "Give it another try before abandoning it. I think you might be closer to a solution than it seems."

Another try? "Do I have to find a third child

to teach persistence to both Stanley and Natalie?"

"What do you think, little angel?"

"I'm not sure. Both Natalie and Stanley are persistent about some things, even if they aren't persistent about others. So that gives me an idea."

The archangel smiled. "More finger snapping?"

"I think so."

Balance

Mr. Moscatelli walked down the aisle handing out all the papers from the week: the fraction test, the science drawing, and the social studies homework.

Stanley had done fine on the fraction test and the social studies homework. But now he looked at his drawing of the wheelbarrow. The grade at the top was just a check. Beside it Mr. Moscatelli had written, "Try something a little more complicated next time."

Stanley folded the drawing fast and lay it on his desk. He looked down so his eyes wouldn't meet anyone else's. Then he turned around and unzipped his backpack, which was hanging from his chair. He went to stuff his drawing in the inner pocket—but it wasn't on his desk anymore.

"Here." Natalie held out Stanley's drawing.

Stanley snatched it and folded it again. "Why'd you take it?"

"I didn't. Somehow it landed on my desk. As though there was a wind or something. But the window isn't even open." Natalie lifted both her shoulders, then dropped them. "It came unfolded on its own. I swear."

Stanley glanced over on Natalie's desk. Her science drawing had a star on top.

Natalie looked from her drawing to Stanley. "I love drawing."

"I don't even like drawing."

"Really?"

Stanley was about to say yes, when he felt a yank on his ear. "Ouch."

"What happened?" said Natalie.

Stanley rubbed his ear. "I do like drawing. I'm just not good at art."

"I do art all the time," said Natalie. "I paint and draw. And I make things out of this really nice clay called fimo. And I string bead jewelry. And all sorts of things like that." She folded her papers and put them in her backpack. "I do art as much as you hang from the rings."

"I love the rings," said Stanley.

"Well, I don't even like them," said Natalie. "Ouch." She put her hand over her ear. "Who did that?"

"What?"

Natalie knit her brows. "My ear hurts."

The school bell rang.

Stanley put his drawing in his backpack. "See you Monday."

Stanley opened the door and sat on the floor.

Casper landed on his head and did a little dance.

Stanley laughed.

"You're so cheerful, Stanley," Mamma said. "It must have been a good day."

"Actually," said Stanley, "it wasn't so good. I got back my science drawing." He handed

Mamma the wheelbarrow drawing. "But I did okay on social studies and math." He handed her those papers now.

Mamma looked over all three papers. Then she squatted beside Stanley. "Nice work in social studies and math. Both stars. Shall we celebrate? We could rent a funny video for tonight."

"Aren't you going to say anything about the drawing?"

"I wasn't going to, because you seem so sad. But if you want to talk about it, let's talk." Mamma smiled and tapped Stanley on the nose. "What does Mr. Moscatelli's note here mean?"

"A wheelbarrow's too simple. I started out doing a car clutch." Stanley turned over the drawing. "See? But I messed it up. I'm no good at art."

"I like your clutch," said Mamma. "You're fine at art, Stanley."

"You just say that because you're my

mother. Some people are really good at it. Like Natalie."

"Natalie?" Mamma sat back on her heels. "Tell me about Natalie."

"She has a dog that sounds almost as good as Casper. But she's bad at the rings."

"The monkey bar rings?"

"Yeah."

Mamma smiled. "Well, that's a nice balance. She's good at art—you're good at the rings. And you both love your pets."

"Except it's not balanced," said Stanley. "Because I wish I could get better at art, but she doesn't care about the rings."

"Oh. How do you know?"

"She said so. She's nice. Can I invite her over?"

"Well, okay." Mamma got up and rubbed the back of her knees.

Stanley went to the phone and opened the school directory. He dialed.

"Hello?"

60

"Hello. This is Stanley. May I please speak to Natalie?"

"Hi, Stanley."

"Want to come over?"

"When?" asked Natalie.

"Tomorrow morning."

"Let me ask." There was a short silence. "My father's taking me to the orthodontist at nine," said Natalie, "but I could come after that."

"We have some paints."

"Okay."

"Maybe you could help me paint better."

"Okay," said Natalie. "We can do it for a long time. That way you'll get good."

"Bye." Stanley hung up.

"Well?" said Mamma.

"I've got to clean up the paint set," said Stanley, "so everything's ready."

The phone rang.

"Hello?" said Stanley.

"Hi," said Natalie. "After we paint, can we

go to that playground you talked about? The one with the rings?"

"Okay," said Stanley.

Natalie was silent.

Finally, Stanley understood. "We can do the rings for a long time, too. You'll get better at them, Natalie."

"Okay. Bye." The line went dead.

Stanley grinned at Mamma.

"Is it celebration time?" asked Mamma.

"Yes. Let's go get a video, like you said. But first I want to give Casper a bath. He loves baths—so that way he can be happy, too."

"Okay." Mamma went to fill a basin with water.

Stanley put out his finger, and Casper jumped from his head onto it. Stanley held the little bird up to his face and rubbed its tummy with his nose. "I'm going to be that person, Casper. Just watch. I'm going to be that person you think I am."

Casper bent his head so that Stanley's nose would rub the back of his neck.

"After art, there's volleyball, and after volleyball, the world. Who knows what I can do if I try?"

Casper made happy little tweets.

Angel Thoughts

The newest Archangel of Persistence stroked his wings lovingly. They had feathered out completely at the telephone ring when Natalie had called Stanley back.

Pulling on Stanley's and Natalie's ears was a lot more drastic than snapping fingers—they had both yelled, "Ouch!" But at least it had worked. Stanley and Natalie were honest with each other now.

Whether or not Stanley was good at art or Natalie was good at the rings might not matter to anyone else in the world, but it mattered to them. And now they were going to work at it. And that had to feel good.

The newest Archangel of Persistence rose

into the air and shook out the tension in his feet. He smiled and flew off to find those tap shoes. After all, he had a lot of hard work ahead, so he better get started.

Read all of the
Aladdin *Angelwings* stories:

№ 1

Friends Everywhere
0-689-82694-X

№ 2

Little Creatures
0-689-82695-8

№ 3

On Her Own
0-689-82985-X

№. 4

One Leap Forward
0-689-82986-8

№. 5

Give and Take
0-689-83205-2

№. 6

No Fair!
0-689-83206-0

And don't miss these other Aladdin *Angelwings* stories:

№ 7
April Flowers
0-689-83207-9

№ 8
Playing Games
0-689-83208-7

№ 9
Lies and Lemons
0-689-83209-5

№. 10

Running Away
0-689-83210-9

№. 11

Know-It-All
0-689-83572-8

№. 12

New Voices
0-689-83573-6

No. 13

Left Out
0-689-83971-5

No. 14

Happy Holidays
0-689-83977-4

No. 15

Partners
0-689-83972-3

All titles $3.99 US / $5.50 Canadian

Aladdin Paperbacks
Simon & Schuster Children's Publishing
www.SimonSaysKids.com

If you like horses, friends, fun, and excitement, then you'll love

Sheltie

The little pony with the big heart!

written and illustrated by Peter Clover

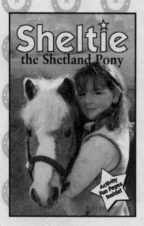

JOIN SHELTIE AND EMMA IN THEIR MANY THRILLING ADVENTURES TOGETHER!

#1 Sheltie the Shetland Pony
0-689-83574-4/$3.99

#2 Sheltie Saves the Day!
0-689-83575-2/$3.99

#3 Sheltie and the Runaway
0-689-83576-0/$3.99

#4 Sheltie Finds a Friend
0-689-83975-8/$3.99

#5 Sheltie to the Rescue
0-689-83976-6/$3.99

#6 Sheltie in Danger
0-689-84028-4/$3.99

Aladdin Paperbacks • Simon & Schuster Children's Publishing
www.SimonSaysKids.com

Lizzie Logan

will make you laugh!

Read all three books:

Lizzie Logan Wears Purple Sunglasses 0-689-81848-3
$3.99 / $5.50 Canadian

Lizzie Logan Gets Married 0-689-82071-2
$3.99 / $5.50 Canadian

Lizzie Logan, Second Banana 0-689-83048-3
$3.99 / $5.50 Canadian

Simon & Schuster Children's Publishing
www.SimonSaysKids.com